HarperCollins*Publishers*

First published in hardback by HarperCollins Publishers Inc, USA in 1991
First published in hardback in Great Britain by HarperCollins Publishers Ltd in 2002
First published in paperback by Collins Picture Books in 2002

1 3 5 7 9 10 8 6 4 2

ISBN: 0-00-712838-X

Collins Picture Books is an imprint of the Children's Division,
part of HarperCollins Publishers Ltd.

Text copyright © Laura Joffe Numeroff 1991
Illustrations copyright © Felicia Bond 1991
The author and illustrator assert the moral right to
be identified as the author and illustrator of the work.
A CIP catalogue record for this title is available from the British Library.
All rights reserved. No part of this publication may be reproduced, stored in a
retrieval system or transmitted in any form or by any means, electronic, mechanical,
photocopying, recording or otherwise, without the prior permission of HarperCollins
Publishers Ltd, 77-85 Fulham Palace Road, Hammersmith, London W6 8JB.

The HarperCollins website address is: www.fireandwater.com

Manufactured in China

For Alice and Emily, the two best sisters
anyone could ever possibly want!

L.J.N.

For Antoine, Nahem, Jennifer, Santos, Brian and Crystal

F.B.

If you give a moose a muffin,

he'll want some jam to go with it.

So you'll bring out some of your mother's home-made blackberry jam.

When he's finished eating
the muffin, he'll want another.

And another.

And another.
When they're all gone,
he'll ask you to make more.

You'll have to go to the shop
to get some muffin mix.

He'll want to go with you.

When he opens the door and feels how chilly it is, he'll ask to borrow a cardigan.

When he puts the cardigan on, he'll notice one of the buttons is loose.

He'll ask for a needle and thread.

He'll start sewing.
The button will remind him of the
puppets his grandmother
used to make.

So he'll ask for some old socks.

He'll make sock puppets.

When they're done, he'll want to put on a puppet show.

He'll need some cardboard
and paints.

Then he'll ask you to help make the scenery.

When the scenery is finished, he'll get behind the couch.
But his antlers will stick out.

So he'll ask for something to cover them up.

You'll bring him a sheet from your bed.

When he sees the sheet, he'll remember
he wants to be a ghost for Halloween.

He'll try it on and shout,

"BOO!"

It'll scare him
so much, he'll knock
over the paints.

So he'll use the sheet
to clean up the mess.

Then he'll ask for some soap to wash it out.

He'll probably want to hang the sheet up to dry.

He'll go outside to put it on the clothesline.

When he's out in the garden, he'll see
your mother's blackberry bushes.

Seeing the blackberries
will remind him of
her jam.

He'll probably ask you for some.

And chances are . . .

if you give him the jam,

he'll want a muffin to go with it.